HOORAY JOSÉ!

WRITTEN AND ILLUSTRATED

BY

MICHAEL GARLAND

MARSHALL CAVENDISH CHILDREN

Marshall Cavendish Corporation
99 White Plains Road, Tarrytown, NY 10591
www.marshallcavendish.us

Library of Congress Cataloging-in-Publication Data

Garland, Michael, 1952-
Hooray José! / written and illustrated by Michael Garland. -- 1st ed.
p. cm.
Summary: Because he is such a short mouse, José is never picked to play basketball, but his determination to play well and a lot of practice
get him on the team and give him the ability to step in when the star player is injured the day of the playoffs.
ISBN-13: 978-0-7614-5345-1
[1. Basketball--Fiction. 2. Determination (Personality trait)--Fiction. 3. Size--Fiction. 4. Mice--Fiction. 5. Stories in rhyme.] I. Title.

PZ8.3.G185Hoo 2007
[E]--dc22

2006022274

The text of this book is set in Worcester.
The illustrations are rendered in Photoshop.

Book design by MichaelNelsonDesign
Printed in Malaysia

First edition
1 3 5 6 4 2

mc **Marshall Cavendish**
Children

To my friend José Ortiz

–M. G.

JOSÉ WAS A SMALL MOUSE WITH BIG BASKETBALL DREAMS.
The Knicks and the Lakers were *his* favorite teams.
But down at the park, on the basketball court,
no one picked him to play, because he was *short*!

They practiced without him; it just wasn't fair.
So he played by himself and tried not to care.
He worked on his dribble. He polished his game.
"Just wait and see. They'll *all* know my name!"

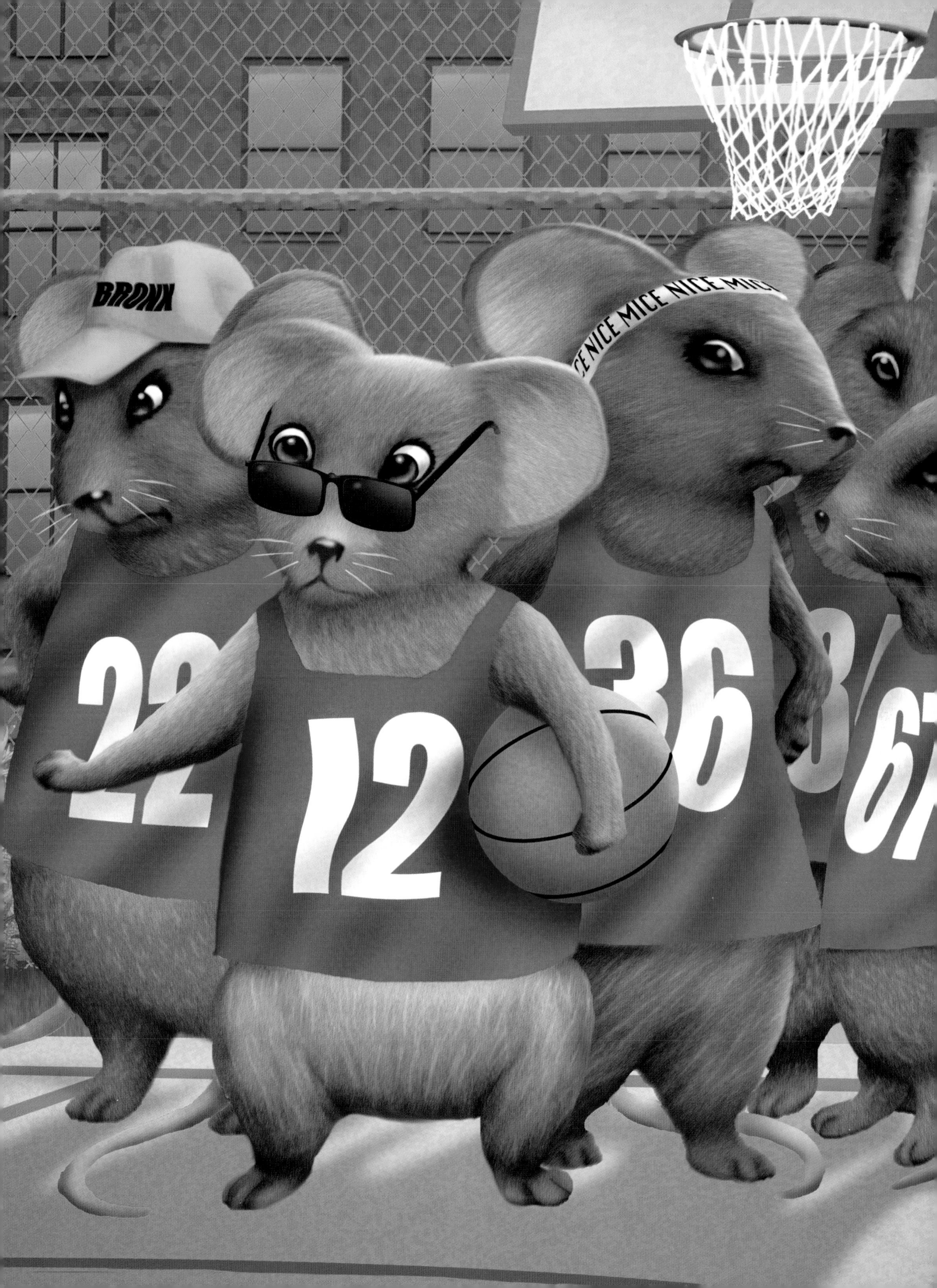
BRONX
NICE MICE NICE MICE
22
12
36
67

He picked up his game with some tricky new shots.
His crossover fake-out could tie you in knots.
He perfected his drive as well as his hook.
You couldn't count up all the foul shots he took.

All José wanted was to play with the Mice.
He pleaded and begged, "Why can't you be nice?"

He wore them all down till they started to scream,
"O-*kaaay*, José! You can be on the team!"

But during their games, José sat on the side,
watching the Mice as they won, lost, or tied.
If someone got hurt, José wanted to play,
but that never happened, so he waited each day.

The Mice played the Chipmunks, all but José.
Stuck on the bench, he still did not play.

Squirrels versus Mice, it was more of the same.
Hamsters and Gerbils—he sat out each game.

Of all the Mice players, Felix played the best.
In the match with the Moles, he was put to the test.
Felix twisted his ankle; José thought he would play.
Though Felix limped badly, he refused to give way.

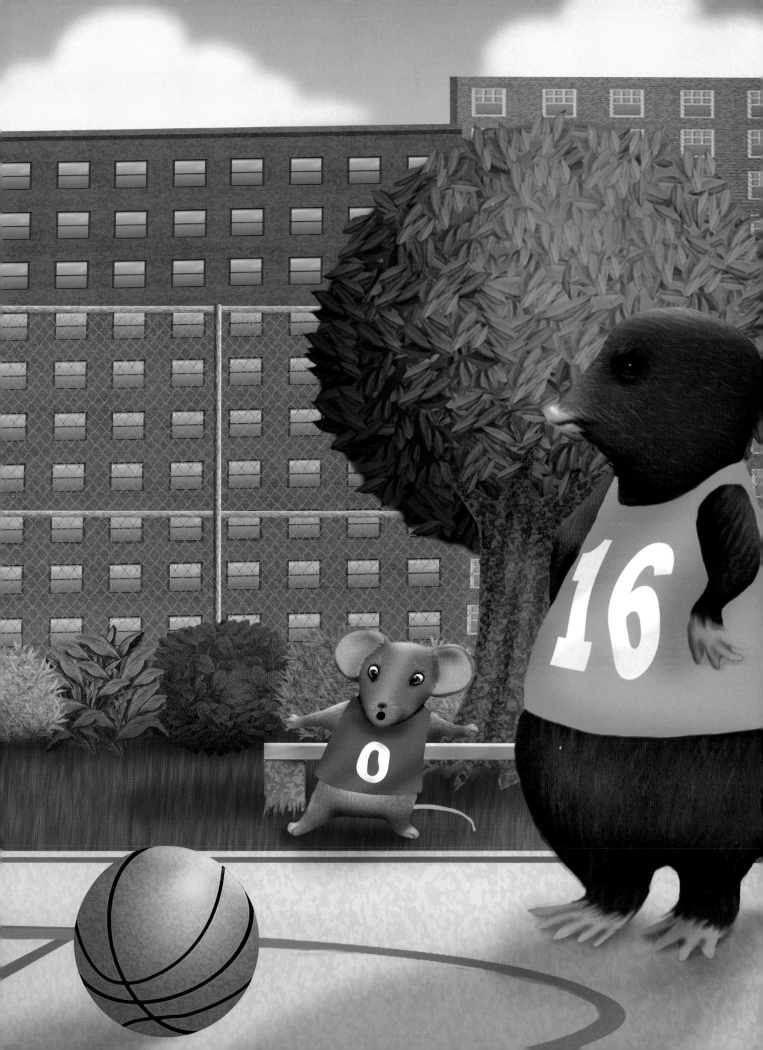

It was Championship Day with a trophy to win.
Mice versus Rats, let the contest begin!

On the way to the park, the Mice suddenly stopped.
Their mouths opened wide, their eyeballs all popped.

A really big mousetrap sat baited with cheese.
José was smart. He yelled, "Stop, Mice, freeze!"
But Felix was starving; he just couldn't wait.
Then he got slammed when he dove for the bait!

Felix was out; there was no chance he could play.
"At last," said José, "it's finally my day!"

"Okay, little mouse, let's see what you've got.
"Step out on the court and take
your best shot!"

It was a very close game with time running out.
No one passed him the ball; José started to shout.

"I'm open! I'm open!" his team heard him call.
"The Mice *have* to score now! Just give me the ball!"

A Rat blocked a pass; it bounced to José.
"This is my chance! It's my turn to play!"

He raced down the court with lightning fast speed.
"My slam jam will score the points that we need."

There was only one Rat between him and the hoop.
Now was the time for an alley-oop scoop.
With his tail like a corkscrew, he bounced high in the air.
He flew toward the basket like he was climbing a stair.

José soared past the Rat and stuffed the ball in.
High fives all around for the greatest Mouse win!

The team lifted José. They raised him up high.
Three cheers for a mouse that would never say die!

HOORAY! HOORAY! HOORAY, JOSÉ!

HOORAY! HOORAY! HOORAY, JOSÉ!